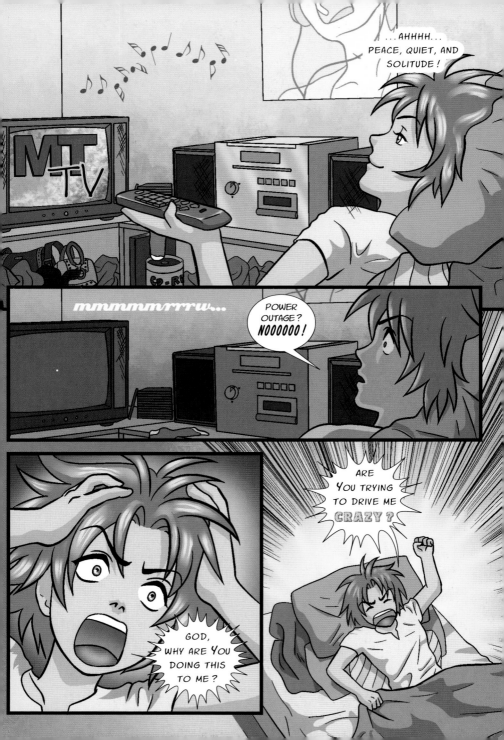

FIRST GET MORE LIGHT IN HERE, THEN FIGURE OUT WHAT TO DO ...

... RAIN ...

... WATER ...

... WET ...

YEAH, IT'S NOTHING BUT A BUNCHA STUPID OLD "THOU SHALT NOTS" BUT...

...RIGHT NOW IT'S THE ONLY ENTERTAINMENT I'VE GOT!

'SIDES, ISN'T THERE A BUNCHA X-RATED STUFF IN THE BIBLE?

LET'S SEE WHAT I CAN FIND!

HOW'RE YOU DOING?

MOM?
WHY ARE YOU BACK SO EARLY?

"EARLY?!?!"
SERENITY, I HAD TO WORK LATE!

MOM ...
WHADDYA
KNOW ABOUT
THE BIBLE ?

"THE BIBLE ?"
IT'S JUST A BUNCHA
OLD STUFF.

BUT,
ISN'T IT LIKE ...
IMPORTANT
AND STUFF ?
Y'KNOW, FOR
SPIRITUAL
GROWTH OR
WHATEVER ...?

* Serenity #2

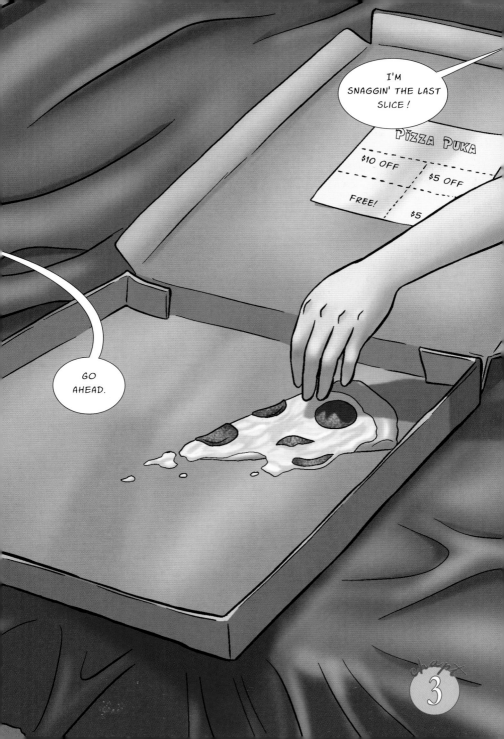

DO YOU FEEL ANYTHING WHEN YOU DO?

YEAH -- STUPID!

...UH...NOT REALLY...

SOMETIMES WE WONDER WHY GOD DOESN'T ANSWER PRAYERS IMMEDIATELY...

LIKE HEALING MOM!

LIKE DRIVING THOSE THOUGHTS OUTTA MY HEAD!

BUT YA GOTTA KEEP PRAYING!

GOD ANSWERS EVERY HEARTFELT PRAYER!

HE JUST MAY SAY "NOT YET."

Wednesday evening, after doctor's appointment . . .

OKAY IF I GO OUT TONIGHT?

YOU BROKE YOUR LEG -- NOW YOU WANNA *AGGRAVATE* IT BY *PARTYING!*

MY ONLY *AGGRAVATION* -- OH, SKIP IT! CAN I GO, YES OR NO?

DO WHAT YOU WANT!

JUST DON'T EXPECT ME TO DRIVE!

THE GERUNDING

MAYBE IT AIN'T WORTH BEING A CHRISTIAN IF I CAN'T YELL BACK!

STILL ... SHE DIDN'T SAY I COULDN'T GO ...

NOT THAT IT WOULD MATTER IF SHE DID!

BUT WHAT ABOUT ALL THOSE "THOU SHALT NOTS ...?"

READ MATTHEW 22:36-39.

flip-flip-flip

TRY THE NEW TESTAMENT ...

flip-flip-flip

I KNOW, KIMBERLY!

Matthew 22:37-39 NIV

FOR THAT MATTER, WHO BELIEVES THAT LOVE STUFF?

=sigh= I KNOW I'D LIKE TO!

DEREK! CHECK OUT KJ52 MP3!

SOLID!

THERE'S DEREK -- AND NO KIMBERLY!

EL PERFECT-O!

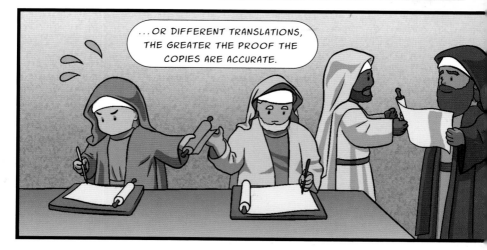

Philippians 2:11 (NIV)

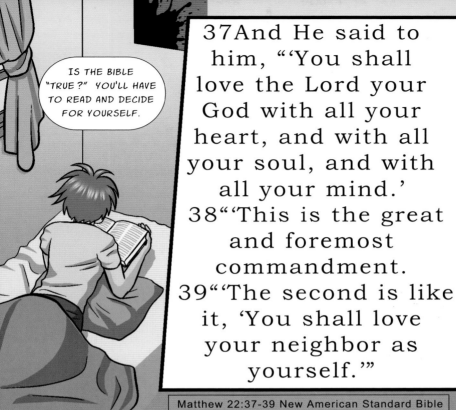

"You shall love"

KIMBERLY CALVIN -- *the early years*

FOR THE ORIGINAL Serenity MAGAZINE PROPOSAL, KIMBERLY
WAS THE BIOLOGICAL DAUGHTER OF ROSS AND JENNIFER CALVIN.
WHEN Serenity BECAME A SERIES OF GRAPHIC NOVELS,
WE RE-DID HER CHARACTER AS AN ASIAN ADOPTEE.
FOR MORE Serenity FACTS AND FUN VISIT:

WWW.SERENITYBUZZ.COM

OR

WWW.REALBUZZSTUDIOS.COM

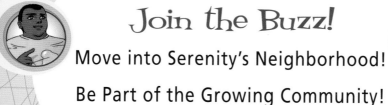

THERE'S A REASON AND A PURPOSE BEHIND EVERYTHING THE PRAYER CLUB DOES!
HERE'S WHERE THEY FIND GUIDANCE AND MEANING FOR THEIR LIVES:

"SO IS MY WORD THAT GOES OUT
FROM MY MOUTH: IT WILL NOT
RETURN TO ME EMPTY, BUT WILL
ACCOMPLISH WHAT I DESIRE AND
ACHIEVE THE PURPOSE FOR WHICH
I SENT IT."

Isaiah 55:11
(New International Version)

"BUT THESE ARE WRITTEN
THAT YOU MAY BELIEVE
THAT JESUS IS THE CHRIST,
THE SON OF GOD, AND
THAT BY BELIEVING YOU
MAY HAVE LIFE IN HIS
NAME."

John 20:31 (NIV)

"ASK AND IT WILL BE GIVEN TO YOU; SEEK
AND YOU WILL FIND; KNOCK AND THE
DOOR WILL BE OPENED TO YOU."

Matthew 7:7 (NIV)

and **Verse**

"I DO BELIEVE; HELP ME
OVERCOME MY UNBELIEF!"
Mark 9:24 (NIV)

"...YOU WILL KNOW THE TRUTH, AND THE
TRUTH WILL SET YOU FREE."

John 8:32 (NIV)

"I WRITE THESE THINGS TO YOU WHO BELIEVE IN THE
NAME OF THE SON OF GOD SO THAT YOU MAY KNOW
THAT YOU HAVE ETERNAL LIFE."

1 John 5:13 (NIV)

BOTTOM LINE:
"THAT IF YOU CONFESS WITH YOUR MOUTH,
'JESUS IS LORD,' AND BELIEVE IN YOUR
HEART THAT GOD RAISED HIM FROM THE
DEAD, YOU WILL BE SAVED. FOR IT IS WITH
YOUR HEART THAT YOU BELIEVE AND ARE
JUSTIFIED, AND IT IS WITH YOUR MOUTH THAT
YOU CONFESS AND ARE SAVED. AS THE
SCRIPTURE SAYS, 'ANYONE WHO TRUSTS IN
HIM WILL NEVER BE PUT TO SHAME.'"
Romans 10:9-11 (NIV)

SERENITY™

ART BY MIN KWON

CREATED BY BUZZ DIXON

ORIGINAL CHARACTER DESIGNS
BY DRIGZ ABROT

SERENITY THROWS A BIG WET SLOPPY ONE OUT TO:
NANCY D.H., CHARLOTTE B.H., KEVIN M., AND LYNN F.

LUV U GUYZ !!!

Copyright © 2006 by Realbuzz Studios, Inc.

ISBN 1-59310-875-3

Published by Barbour Publishing, Inc., P.O. Box 719, Uhrichsville, Ohio 44683
www.barbourbooks.com

"OUR MISSION IS TO PUBLISH AND DISTRIBUTE INSPIRATIONAL PRODUCTS OFFERING EXCEPTIONAL VALUE AND BIBLICAL ENCOURAGEMENT TO THE MASSES."

 Member of the
Evangelical Christian
Publishers Association

Scripture quotations marked NIV are taken from The HOLY BIBLE, NEW INTERNATIONAL VERSION®. NIV®. Copyright © 1973, 1978, 1984 by International Bible Society. Used by permission of Zondervan. Scripture taken from the NEW AMERICAN STANDARD BIBLE © 1960, 1962, 1963, 1968, 1971, 1972, 1973, 1975, 1977 by the Lockman Foundation. Used by permission. All rights reserved.

Printed in China.
5 4 3 2 1

VISIT *SERENITY* AT:
www.Serenitybuzz.com
www.RealbuzzStudios.com